GRAND TETON NATIONAL PARK
To the Top of the Grand

Adventures with the Parkers

Mike Graf

ILLUSTRATED BY
Marjorie Leggitt

FALCONGUIDES

GUILFORD, CONNECTICUT
HELENA, MONTANA
AN IMPRINT OF GLOBE PEQUOT PRESS

FALCONGUIDES®

Text © 2013 Mike Graf
Illustrations © 2013 Marjorie Leggitt

FalconGuides is an imprint of Globe Pequot Press.
Falcon, FalconGuides, and Outfit Your Mind are registered trademarks of Morris Book
Publishing, LLC.

Illustrations: Marjorie Leggitt
Models for twins: Amanda and Ben Frazier

Photos by Mike Graf and Kimberly Alexander Graf with the following exceptions, which are
licensed by Shutterstock.com: inset p. i © Lukasz Bizon; p. 1 © Steve Bower; p. 5 © Sascha
Burkard; p. 9 © Mike Norton; p. 10 © Steve Estvanik; p. 18 © Wildphoto3; p. 20 © Tony
Campbell; p. 22 © Kimberley McClard; p. 23 top © Darlene Cutshall; p. 23 bottom © Steve
Adamson; p. 25 bottom © Daniel Rose; p. 26 top © Debbie Steinhausser; p. 26 bottom ©
Tom Reichner; p. 29 top © Ronnie Howard; p. 29 bottom © Greg A. Boiarsky; p. 30 ©
Tucker James; p. 32 © Glenn R. McGloughlin; p. 38 © Jack Sorensen; p. 39 © gimsy; p. 41,
78, 84 © Exum Guides; p. 42 © swinner; p. 46 © Flegere; p. 53 © BMJ; p. 61 © Wang Chi-
Jui; pp. 64, 69 © Rick Laverty; p. 73 © Jerry Sanchez; p. 82 © Tom Grundy; p. 85 © Zack C;
p. 91 © Georgy Markov; p. 94/inside back cover © Christina Tisi-Kramer

Map courtesy of National Park Service

Project editor: Julie Marsh
Layout: Melissa Evarts

Library of Congress Cataloging-in-Publication Data

Graf, Mike.
Grand Teton National Park : to the top of the Grand / Mike Graf ;
illustrated by Marjorie Leggitt.
pages cm. — (Adventures with the Parkers)
ISBN 978-0-7627-8274-1
1. Grand Teton National Park (Wyo.)—Guidebooks—Juvenile literature.
I. Leggitt, Marjorie. II. Title.
F767.T3G68 2013
978.7'55—dc23
                                                                         2013002919

Printed in the United States of America
10 9 8 7 6 5 4 3 2 1

The Grizzly Adoption

It was a warm summer night at Grand Teton National Park. In the late-evening darkness, a gathering of wildlife onlookers on the deck of Jackson Lake Lodge was slowly dispersing.

One man passed his binoculars to his wife. "The grizzly with the three cubs is still out that way. But it's getting harder and harder to see."

The woman took the binoculars and scanned in the direction where the bears were last seen. She looked for several minutes. "I think they're behind some willows now. Either that or it's too dark. I can't find them."

Another viewer nearby reported, "I've lost track of the other grizzly with two cubs as well. I can't believe we saw them, though."

The Jackson Lake Lodge deck emptied further. Eventually even the silhouettes of the Teton Range could barely be made out against the night sky. By now, most people had gone inside.

Meanwhile the grizzly with the three cubs continued to prowl for food in Willow Flats. The scent of elk and the possibility of surprising a mom with a vulnerable young calf led her south toward the heart of the flatland of marshy thickets.

At the other end of Willow Flats, the grizzly with two cubs followed a similar track. She ambled north to where the possibility of a young elk calf also awaited. Her two cubs followed behind, occasionally stopping at a new scent then scampering to catch up.

A third grizzly entered the area. The large male was seeking a female to mate with. Its powerful sense of smell led it straight into Willow Flats.

All the bears were now, more or less, heading right toward each other. Finally, after the sky was completely black, their paths converged.

The bear with the three cubs stood up, sensing an intruder. Across the way the two-cub mom did the same. Then, seeming to recognize each other, the bear moms dropped down to all four feet and waltzed past each other, barely acknowledging the other's presence, but also acting at ease.

The male bear trotted into the already occupied clearing. For a brief moment, before being observed or sensed, the male noticed one grizzly mother with three cubs and another with two.

Both mother bears heard a branch snap. They immediately honed in on the male bear. The male grizzly instantly dashed toward a stray cub in an attempt to strike it with a fatal blow.

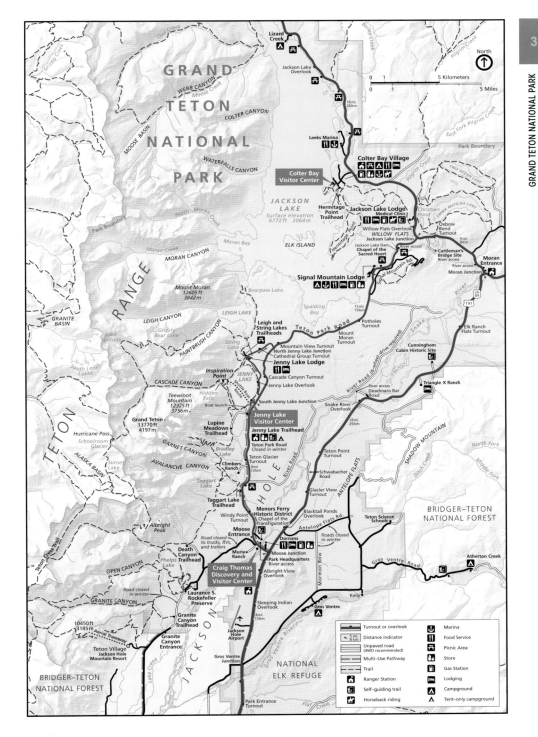

GRAND

TETON

NATIONAL

PARK

TETON

RANGE

JACKSON HOLE

Lizard Creek

Jackson Lake Overlook

16mi 26km

Leeks Marina

Colter Bay Village

Colter Bay Visitor Center

JACKSON LAKE
Surface elevation
6772ft 2064m

Hermitage Point Trailhead

Jackson Lake Lodge
Medical Clinic

Willow Flats Overlook
WILLOW FLATS
Jackson Lake Junction

Oxbow Bend Turnout

5mi 8km

Jackson Lake Dam
Chapel of the Sacred Heart

Cattleman's Bridge Site
River access

River access

Moran Entrance

Moran Junction

Signal Mountain Lodge

12mi 19km

Potholes Turnout

Mount Moran Turnout

ELK ISLAND

Moran Bay

MORAN CANYON

Bearpaw Lake

Spalding Bay

Mount Moran
12605ft 3842m

LEIGH CANYON

LEIGH LAKE

Teton Park Road

Cunningham Cabin Historic Site

Leigh and String Lakes Trailheads

Mountain View Turnout
North Jenny Lake Junction
Cathedral Group Turnout

Jenny Lake Lodge

Cascade Canyon Turnout

Jenny Lake Overlook

Triangle X Ranch

River access
Deadmans Bar Road

PAINTBRUSH CANYON

String Lake

JENNY LAKE

CASCADE CANYON

Inspiration Point

Hidden Falls

Teewinot Mountain
12325ft 3756m

Boat launch

South Jenny Lake Junction

Snake River Overlook

Jenny Lake Visitor Center

Jenny Lake Trailhead

Grand Teton
13770ft 4197m

Lupine Meadows Trailhead

Bradley Lake

Teton Park Road
Closed in winter

Teton Glacier Turnout
8mi 13km

18mi 29km

GARNET CANYON

Climbers Ranch

Teton Point Turnout

Hurricane Pass
Schoolroom Glacier

AVALANCHE CANYON

Taggart Lake

Schwabacher Road

SHADOW MOUNTAIN

North Fork

Middle Fork

Sunset Lake

ALASKA BASIN

Taggart Lake Trailhead

Glacier View Turnout

ANTELOPE FLATS

Ditch Creek

BRIDGER–TETON NATIONAL FOREST

Albright Peak

Windy Point Turnout

Menors Ferry Historic District
Chapel of the Transfiguration

Blacktail Ponds Overlook

Teton Science Schools

Road closed to trucks, RVs, and trailers

Moose Entrance

Dornans

Antelope Flats Rd.

Death Canyon Trailhead

Phelps Lake

Murie Ranch

Moose Junction
Park Headquarters
River access

Roads closed in winter

OPEN CANYON

Road closed in winter

Craig Thomas Discovery and Visitor Center

Albright View Overlook

GRANITE CANYON

Laurance S. Rockefeller Preserve

Sleeping Indian Overlook

Gros Ventre

Gros Ventre Road

Atherton Creek

10450ft 3185m
Aerial Tramway

Granite Canyon Trailhead

Granite Canyon Entrance

8mi 13km

Kelly

Teton Village
Jackson Hole Mountain Resort

Jackson Hole Airport

Gros Ventre Junction

NATIONAL ELK REFUGE

BRIDGER–TETON NATIONAL FOREST

Park Entrance Turnout

Flat Creek

North

0   1   5 Kilometers
0   1   5 Miles

Park Boundary

Owl Creek

WEBB CANYON
Moose Creek

COLTER CANYON

MOOSE BASIN

WATERFALLS CANYON

North Moran Creek

Moran Creek

Park Boundary

GRANITE BASIN

Lake Solitude

Grizzly Bear Lake

South Leigh Lakes

Grizzly Creek

Bailey Creek

Pilgrim Creek

East Fork Pilgrim Creek

TWO OCEAN LAKE

EMMA MATILDA LAKE

Christian Pond

River Rd.

Signal Mountain Rd.

Snake River

River Road (4-wheel-drive required)

26 89

191

Mormon Row

Lake Creek

Gros Ventre River

Turnout or overlook	Marina
Distance indicator	Food Service
Unpaved road (4WD recommended)	Picnic Area
Multi-Use Pathway	Store
Trail	Gas Station
Ranger Station	Lodging
Self-guiding trail	Campground
Horseback riding	Tent-only campground

But the young bear's mother intercepted the attack. She dashed toward the charging male and lunged at it with her teeth bared while bellowing a fearsome growl.

There were still a few visitors strolling around outside on the deck of the lodge. One, taking heed of the spine-chilling roar from somewhere in the flats, froze in her tracks. "Did you hear that?" she shuddered to the others milling about.

The people remaining immediately scanned the darkness and searched the flats with their binoculars. "There were reports of several bears out there earlier," a man said, "but we were at dinner."

A moment later there was another spine-chilling growl.

"There it is again!" the woman exclaimed. "I'm sure glad I'm up here and not out there." She and the others searched the vast darkness but couldn't see anything.

The male bear continued to dash at the young cubs while the mother bears did their best to defend their offspring, repeatedly chasing the menacing predator away.

Finally, in a desperate attempt to kill a young bear, the male ran full speed at the three cubs, dispersing them in different directions.

In the confusion of the darkness and panic from the charge, a bear cub from the family of three found the two cubs from the other mom. In a split second the cub joined the other family and they sprinted away from the violent intruder, soon finding safety and isolation in a distant thicket of willows.

The remaining two cubs with their mom ran in the opposite direction until they were no longer being pursued.

The male bear whirled around, searching for the vanished cubs. But finding nothing, it loped toward a distant grove of trees.

All was now quiet again in Willow Flats. Finally, the last of the lodge visitors strolled up the stairs and into the lodge. She whispered to herself, "I wonder what was going on out there tonight."

Saddle Up

The Parker family was driving home from their summer vacation.

"This is Morgan Parker with my twin brother, James, my Dad, Robert, and my Mom, Kristen," Morgan said into a tape recorder. "We are going to be talking into this recorder to remember everything we can about our summer. James and I have been to a bunch of national parks, and we have several Junior Ranger badges to prove it. But nothing we've ever experienced in the past compares to our adventures in Grand Teton National Park in Wyoming. We can't wait to talk about it.

"Our trip is over now and we are on our long drive home to California across the Nevada desert, so there's plenty of time to reflect. And there's a lot on our minds about the Tetons—we are already homesick about leaving. Both James and I don't know where to begin sharing our journey."

Morgan turned off the tape recorder. "So where should we start?" she asked, looking at her family.

"You could just tell the story in order," Dad suggested from the front.

"But the days just seem to blend together when looking back," James said. "I hope we can remember how it all went."

"Dad is right, I think," Mom said. "It is best to tell the events in the truest order we can."

"Then the horseback ride and the grizzlies should go first," Morgan decided.

"Yeah, that's a good place to start," James agreed. *"But just don't leave out any good details!"*

"Like 399," Mom called out.

"Or the carcass," Dad added.

"Don't worry, it's all right in here," Morgan pointed to her head, and with that she pressed record.

"So let's saddle up and go for a ride in the Tetons . . . "

"OK, James, step on over," the wrangler called.

James walked up to Pam, the wrangler, and hopped onto a step stool. Then he hoisted himself onto Foxy, his horse. James grabbed the saddle, shifted his weight to the center of the horse, and grinned.

"Morgan Parker, you're next," Pam announced.

Morgan waltzed up to her horse. "What's her name?"

"Pig Pen," Pam replied. "But don't worry, she's actually very clean. We opposite named her."

Morgan smiled at her animal companion and stroked her mane. "Hi, Pig Pen, old buddy. I can't wait to go for a ride."

Morgan hopped onto the booster step, lifted her foot into a stirrup, and hoisted herself up.

After a few adjustments and some last-minute instructions, such as "pull back on the reins and say 'whoa' when you want her to stop, and let the reins go as a reward if she listens" and "show her you're the boss," the Parkers were all set to go.

Pam led the Parkers along a pathway under the highway. Morgan's horse kept getting too close to James's. The riders had been instructed to keep the animals a horse length apart. "Hold on, Pig Pen, slow down!" Morgan called out. When the horse obeyed, Morgan said, "Nice job. There you go."

Pam told the group that she has been riding horses since she was ten. *This is only my third time on a horse,* Morgan thought to herself. But it's the first one in open terrain. The other times were all in fenced-in arenas.

Somewhere early on the trek, Dad, who rode in front, turned around. "How are you two doing back there?" he called out to the twins. Then he shifted his attention to the mountains to the west. "Well," Dad said with awe. "Would you look at that! The Teton mountains are piercing the sky!"

Mom, in the back, added, "They're stunning." Then she snapped a picture of the family moseying along.

"I can't believe we're going to be climbing that!" Dad said, referring to the tallest mountain in the range.

James commented, "It looks like the top of the world."

Mom glanced down and called out excitedly. "I think I just saw wolf scat along the trail!"

Pam heard Mom. "There are wolves around here. But they're also pretty elusive. We see signs of them much more often than we actually get to spot a wolf."

Pam started telling the group about the area. "Willow Flats, the marshy fields just below Jackson Lake Lodge, is closed to people. Elk are in there now, and the mothers are dropping calves. But the grizzles know it. And they're scouring the thickets, searching for an easy meal. It just isn't safe for people in there."

Bears nearby, James thought to himself. *How cool is that! Or is it?*

As the group traversed along a marshy area, Pam called out, "Look along that hillside across the way."

She pointed to a pack of brown dots. "Elk!" Dad exclaimed.

James quickly counted. "There are six!" he announced.

"All female. I don't see any with antlers," Morgan added.

The elk heard the group talking. They lifted their heads from grazing and watched the train of horses pass by.

"Pretty cool," Morgan said. "Our first major animal sighting."

"We should keep track of all the animals we see and where," James said to Morgan.

Soon they left the open fields behind and the trail led everyone into the forest. That's when Pam said, "There's another elk up ahead, but this one's in an entirely different condition."

Pam pointed toward the right of the trail. "Up here, in that little pile of thick grass, is an elk carcass, or what's left of it from a wolf or bear killing five years ago. A pile of bleached bones has been there ever since."

As the Parkers passed by what was left of the elk, Morgan noticed what she thought were rib bones. She swallowed nervously and gave Pig Pen a little kick to quicken her pace out of the area. Morgan looked around and wondered how often large predators take down an elk.

Morgan kicked Pig Pen again. Her horse cooperated by breaking into a little trot. "Good job, Pig Pen!" Morgan said, then pulled her reins back to slow down.

The group was in a mixed forest now. White-barked aspen trees were scattered about. Pam took the opportunity to tell everyone a Shoshone

Indian legend about them.

"Aspen trees used to have black bark—as dark as Native American hair. The trees thought their appearance was the most beautiful thing on earth, and they often boasted of their looks. Mother Nature, though, came along and said, 'You have to stop this boasting about how beautiful you are. Everything in nature is equally stunning in its own way.' But the tress couldn't help themselves. They really thought that of all creatures in nature, they were the most pretty, and they kept talking about it.

"Mother Earth came back with an angry storm full of wind, rain, and lightning to punish the trees. This frightened them so much, they turned white with fear and have remained that color to this day. Now, whenever the wind picks up and a storm is coming, the leaves of the aspen tremble with fear, which is why they are called quaking aspen. The trees are afraid Mother Earth is going to come back and destroy them the next time."

As Morgan, James, Mom, and Dad pushed up another hill, Pam shared parts of the park's history.

"Fur trappers first came here for coveted beaver pelts. Beaver hats were in fashion in the big cities, and there was lots of money to be made. Beaver populations were devastated."

"That's so sad," Morgan whispered to James.

"Then the silkworm was discovered in Asia and silk became fashionable, so beavers were mostly forgotten about and gradually their numbers began to increase. That's when cattle ranching became popular here. But grazing cattle was difficult due to harsh weather and rocky soil. Ranchers moved on to dude ranching, where people could come and live on Western-style ranches and do daily routines such as taking care of animals and going horseback riding. That began attracting lots of tourists to the area."

"There's just so much history here," Dad commented.

"In fact," Pam continued, "the Colter Bay cabins are some of the original cabins from the dude-ranching era."

"That's where we are staying!" James said.

Pam told the group more. "But homesteads and shabby buildings and garbage dumps of settlers and entrepreneurs were ruining the land. Horace Albright, then superintendent of Yellowstone, wanted to protect the Tetons and Jackson Hole from further development. He dreamed of preserving the area as a national park, just like Yellowstone, but he knew he needed some help. So in 1924 and 1926, Horace toured Jackson Hole with John D. Rockefeller Jr. and his family to encourage Mr. Rockefeller's help in buying out the offending properties.

"Albright's plan worked. In 1927 Rockefeller, a well-known wealthy conservationist, began buying up chunks of land here, in the Jackson Hole area, but under a fake company, the Snake River Land Company. He didn't want anyone to know he was doing the buying.

"In 1929 the Teton mountain range became a national park, but that didn't include the valley. There were groups of people who did not want the government to take over Jackson Hole's private lands. But in 1943 Franklin Delano Roosevelt, our president at the time, used the Antiquities Act to make Jackson Hole a national monument, utilizing some of the land donated by Rockefeller. In 1950 that area was added to the national park and covers the land as we see it today. But it was a long, hard-fought battle."

"Well, it was certainly worth it," Mom mused.

"Some of the people who opposed the park later admitted that it was the best thing that ever happened to the area," Pam added.

The group fell into a quiet rhythm and soon arrived at massive Emma Matilda Lake. "The lake is named after William Owen's wife," Pam told everyone. "Owen is claimed to be one of the first people to climb the Grand Teton, and he saw this lake from up there."

Pam guided the riders a few feet off the trail. Immediately, as if on cue, Pig Pen and the other horses dropped their heads and began grazing. "I can see you're hungry," Morgan said while petting her horse. "Go ahead and eat some."

Soon they were on their way again, and they began overlooking a course of water. "That's Oxbow Bend down there," Pam pointed out. "And those white dots on the water are either trumpeter swans or white pelicans. They are too far away to know for sure, but you should head down there one evening. It's one of the best places in the park to see wildlife."

As the group moved west, the Teton mountain range was always within view. "What an incredible sight," Mom said.

Pam had the horses stop. "Photo shoot!" she called out. Pam lined everyone up parallel to each other, and with the Parkers' camera, snapped a picture for the family.

"I bet that'll end up on our hallway wall!" James exclaimed.

After a few more ups and downs, Pam led the riders toward a marshy body of water called Christian Pond. While they trotted along, something changed in Pam's body language. She suddenly seemed tense and on high alert, scanning the horizon. As the group climbed along a ridge with views of the entire marshy pond, they soon found out why.

"There are grizzlies across the way," Pam announced.

Everyone saw the bears right away. They were on the other side of the pond. One grizzly, the mother, appeared to be lounging in the sun. At the same time, two cubs were running and chasing each other and splashing in the water. It appeared like simple summer fun.

Pam, a bit more relaxed now seeing how far away the bears were, turned to the group and said, "Those four bears, the mother and her three cubs, have been hanging out for a few weeks now at Christian Pond. We see them nearly every day. It's quite a little bonus for our ride. And they seem to not be fazed by us at all. They're just doing their thing."

One of the cubs now grabbed the other's neck, and they rolled around and tumbled into the marsh. Dad watched with binoculars. "Did you say four bears?" he asked. "I only see three."

"Yes," Pam replied, while gazing out. She watched the two cubs and also spotted the mom. Then she grabbed a pair of binoculars from a pocket on her saddle and scanned the area. "Well, that's odd," she said. "Where's the other cub?"

Pam told the group, "That's bear 399. I can tell for sure by the red tag on her left ear. I also know it's her by the dark line, or scar, across her face and lip. The grizzles in the area are being tagged and monitored. The number they have comes from the order they were tagged."

All four of the Parkers focused in and concentrated on the grizzly's face for quite some time, trying to pick out the battle wound, but couldn't find it.

"Yesterday she was out here with all three of her cubs." Pam fell silent again, searching the area. "This could be very unfortunate."

"What do you mean?" James asked.

"She appears to be missing a cub. Bear cubs could be preyed upon by other bears, or even a wolf. I don't want to even think about it."

Then Pam picked up a cell phone. She called into the stables and reported what they were seeing. "Yes, she only has two cubs. We've been looking for quite a while."

Finally Pam turned to everyone. "We better get back now," she announced, and soon the riders left the three bears behind.

As the group snaked back under the highway and up toward the stables, one of the wranglers came jogging up. "Guess what!?" she exclaimed. "Bear 610 now has three cubs with her!"

"What?" Pam responded.

"Yes, she's been spotted all morning out at Willow Flats."

After the wrangler finished relaying more details, Pam explained to the group. "610 is 399's grown daughter. She had a litter of two cubs, and 399 had three this year. I wonder if they exchanged a cub. It seems that maybe one of 399's cubs has been adopted by 610."

"You mean, 399's cub could be OK then?" James asked.

"I'm not sure," Pam replied. "It seems amazing, but that might be."

Soon afterward the group returned to the safety of the stables. Pam dismounted and with the aid of other wranglers, helped each person off his or her horse. Then Pam came over with a bag of food. "Horse cookies," she called them. Each of the Parkers took one and walked up to their horse. They held their hands flat and let their horse lick the cookie up right out of their palm. After, James wiped his hands on his jeans. "That was fun!" he announced, smiling.

The Laurance S. Rockefeller Preserve

As the Parkers passed Winnemucca and the dry lands of Nevada rolled on, Mom suddenly called out, "I want to tell about the next day at the Laurance S. Rockefeller Preserve. That might have been my favorite part of the park."

"Here, Mom," Morgan said, passing her the tape recorder.

"Thanks, Morgan," Mom said while looking at the nearly plant-less terrain out the window. "Remember how lush and green it was in there?" she recalled.

"Make sure you mention the visitor center," Dad said.

"And don't forget about the Sound Room," James reminded her.

"Or the clucking grouse," Morgan added.

"How could I?" Mom smiled, then pressed RECORD . . .

The Parkers arrived early for their guided hike. A ranger directed them to a parking spot and pointed out the visitor center. Only fifty cars at a time were allowed in the lot, and just ten people could go on the hike; reservations were required.

Jessie, the ranger, introduced herself by saying, "This is my dream job. I can't think of anywhere else I'd rather be."

Jessie went on to tell the Parkers and the few others in the group about the Rockefellers and how they originally bought this land from the JY Ranch and used it as a family retreat.

The first stop the group made was at a beautiful, tall, healthy quaking aspen tree. James whispered to Morgan, "I wonder if we're going to hear that Shoshone Indian legend again."

Then Jessie pointed out bear claw marks all along the trunk of the tree.

"How did they get way up there?" Morgan asked, seeing claw marks well beyond the reach of any bear.

"They're scars from the tree's younger days," the ranger replied.

"Apparently bears have liked this tree for a long time," Mom said.

The group walked on along the forested pathway. Morgan and James kept looking at other trees for more bear claw markings. Soon they came to a platform for viewing gurgling Lake Creek.

"Lake Creek water is on a grand journey," Jessie told the group. "It starts as snow and ice up in the Tetons. After melting, the water tumbles down the canyons and pours into Phelps Lake. From there it runs down Lake Creek here and all the way to the Snake River. Eventually the Snake River deposits the water into the Columbia River, which takes it all the way to the Pacific Ocean."

"That's quite a *long* journey," James remarked.

Morgan saw a leaf from a nearby aspen tree fall into the creek. "Just think," she announced, "someday that leaf might make it all the way to the Pacific Ocean."

Jessie smiled and said, "It does make you reflect on how well all of nature is connected, doesn't it?"

Jessie led everyone on. At one point she stopped to demonstrate some tree identification techniques.

Jessie called James over first. "Shake the hand, or branch, of this tree here. Touch the needles. Are they soft or pokey?"

James felt the needles and reported, "They're soft."

Jessie responded, "This tree, then, is a 'friendly fir.' The needles are flat; they don't roll well. So we call it a 'flat friendly fir.'"

Next she brought Morgan to help out. "Here, try this one."

Morgan grabbed a branch of needles on another tree. She gripped firmly, then slowly pulled away, letting the needles slide through her hand. "This one has pokey needles," she said.

"We call it a 'spiky spruce,'" the ranger said. "The needles are square, allowing them to roll a little. So it's a square, spiky spruce."

Finally the ranger took the group up to a third type of tree. She picked up a needle from it off the ground. "See these needles? They come in pairs to a point and make an L shape, like their name. These are lodgepole pines."

The ranger continued, "Those are the three most common trees we'll see out here, although there are some others around like whitebark pines, which typically live higher up."

"These are some good techniques to know," Mom said. "Thanks for the tips."

Jessie smiled at Mom. "Glad I could help!"

Soon the group came upon a pile of elk droppings along the trail. James looked into the forest and called out, "The elk are over there!"

There were two female elk about a hundred feet away in the trees.

They looked at the group, and Morgan, James, Mom, and Dad looked at them.

"They seem so content," Dad said.

"They live in a very special place," Mom replied.

The hikers kept a relaxed pace through the preserve. It allowed the group to feel as though they were in their own little world and there was no reason to hurry along. Everyone stopped, though, when Morgan saw a brightly colored bird up in a tree. It was shockingly yellow-breasted and had a red head, making the Parkers think of a tropical bird.

"That's a western tanager," Jessie informed Morgan and the others.

Soon they came upon another unique bird sighting. Jessie pointed out an especially tall tree with a large nest at the top. "It's an eagle's nest!" James exclaimed.

But the ranger informed them, "It's actually an osprey nest. Ospreys return to their nest year after year, so we know they're around, although I haven't seen them lately. Ospreys are one of the three hundred species of birds found in the park."

A little while later, the guided hike came to an open sagebrush meadow. Here the ranger told the group, "This is where the Rockefellers' stables were. They were taken out once this area was made into a preserve. Biologists estimate it will take about eighty years for the area to completely recover."

Morgan stopped and pointed out something that the family had been seeing all over the park. They were nests of caterpillars clinging to bushes in webbed enclosures.

"They're tent caterpillars," the ranger informed the group. "They crawl out during the day to eat and go back in at night."

"Here's one right on the trail," Morgan said.

The group stepped over the little bug and walked on.

Soon the group arrived at the trail's major destination, Phelps Lake. The beautiful mountain body of water was framed by forests, with Death Canyon and snowcapped Albright Peak in the distance. It was a scene of exquisite beauty and grand solitude.

"We're not the only animals that like the area," the ranger said. "Two wolves were spotted denning in the forest nearby, and sometimes backpackers around here are lucky enough to hear them howling at night."

"We're in the vicinity of great carnivores," Dad said in awe.

Jessie provided some more history to the group. They learned that the rocky, flat area where they now stood was once the site of a cabin belonging to the JY Ranch. The ranger then said good-bye, adding, "You are free to walk either of the trails back on your own."

The Parkers decided to stay a while and soak in more of the beauty and solitude. Nearby was a small, sandy area at the shore. It turned out to be a perfect picnic spot.

Mom stopped telling the story and looked at everyone in the car. "How long did we end up staying there?"

"A couple of hours at least," James said.

Dad added, "Yeah, it was so calm and remote."

"It was hard to leave," Morgan said.

Mom continued, "When we all came to, we decided to take the Woodland Trail back to make a loop out of the hike."

On the way down the trail, a bizarre, loud clucking sound came from somewhere in the forest. The Parkers froze in their tracks.

"What was that?" Morgan asked, bewildered.

A sleek, furry carnivore zigzagged across the trail, holding a white egg in its mouth. The egg thief dashed into the forest, when the clucking began again. Instantly a grayish bird tore across the trail, with its feathers ruffled and a few flying in the air behind it. The angry bird chased right after the bandit. Both animals disappeared for a few seconds in the trees, although the clucking continued.

"I think that was a pine marten being chased by a ruffed grouse," Mom said.

"I wonder if it will get its egg back," James added.

Then the marten reappeared, dashing up a tree with the egg in its mouth. The grouse circled the base of the tree, clucking and calling up to the thief.

Once near the treetop, the marten disappeared behind some branches. A moment later, the Parkers could see stray pieces of eggshell shower down onto the grouse and the forest floor.

At that point, Mom whispered over the din of the still-cackling grouse, "I can't believe we got to witness that! But let's leave nature alone now, OK?"

Finally the Parkers finished the hike and made their way into the preserve's unique visitor center. There was a reading library with tables and chairs, and other rooms that had spacious displays and pictures. But most notably there was serenity, just like the trails outside.

"What I remember most, though, are these words." Mom pulled out a little piece of paper and read a quote from Laurance S. Rockefeller. "How we treat our land, how we build upon it, how we act toward our air and water, will in the long run tell us what kind of people we really are."

Mom looked at James, telling him she still remembered. "Of course, our last few minutes there were spent in the circular Sound Room. We listened to the preserve through the speakers: rain, thunder, wind, elk and bird calls, among other recorded sounds."

"It really was a special place!" Mom concluded.

An Evening at Oxbow Bend

The family was smack dab in the middle of their drive west across Nevada. Dad popped open his eyes while appearing to nap in the passenger seat and called out, "Hey—I want to reminisce about Oxbow Bend!"

"I think it was our second evening in the Tetons. We'd heard that Grand Teton National Park was the number one national park in the country for seeing wildlife. So we had to go find out.

"We drove toward the lookout on the Snake River, when Mom said, "We're not going back to our cabin tonight until we have at least ten separate animal sightings.'"

"Ten!?" I echoed. "That's quite a lofty goal!"

But as soon as we drove up, I knew we had a chance.

The parking lot was full of cars. "Something's out there!" Dad announced with anticipation.

It was around 7:45 p.m. and still plenty light out. The crowd of onlookers was peering toward the water and the opposite shore clearing. The Parkers piled out of the car.

"It's a herd of elk!" Morgan cried, pointing to the river and the sagebrush flats beyond.

James lifted the binoculars to his eyes and immediately counted. "There are seven of them!"

"Did you get that one way off by itself?" Morgan asked, pointing.

"Oops, eight," James corrected.

Dad took the binoculars from James and fixed his gaze on the solitary animal. "That one's not an elk," he reported. "It's a pronghorn!"

"OK, seven elk, then, and one pronghorn," James said.

The elk were wading in the water or grazing near the shore.

Then Mom looked in a different direction. "Look! There are some trumpeter swans," she said. Four of them gently glided along the water. They were a stark white, like snow, with long, gracefully arched necks.

"There are more birds over there," James suddenly reported. He directed the family to a small inlet of water where a flock of ducks also inhabited Oxbow Bend. And near them were also several Canada geese.

Mom silently counted on her fingers. "That's five sightings," she said. "We're already halfway there."

The Parkers decided to take the little dirt path closer to the river. There were people down there as well, some even in lounge chairs.

Pronghorn are North America's fastest land animal. They can run up to sixty miles per hour and can keep above thirty mph for miles. There are pronghorn all over the western states, and up to a half million live in Wyoming alone. But the Grand Teton National Park pronghorn are in jeopardy, with only two hundred left, due to oil, gas, and housing developments along their 150-mile-long migration route.

Pronghorn cannot live in the Jackson Hole area during winter because deep snow and subzero temperatures are too severe for their survival. They must migrate along a traditional route, as they have done for over six thousand years. Without this migratory pathway, pronghorns would cease to exist within Grand Teton National Park. Due to this, the National Park Service, USDA Forest Service, and National Elk Refuge are working together to protect the "Path of the Pronghorn" by limiting development and keeping a route available for these animals to migrate to and from the park seasonally.

THE PATH OF THE PRONGHORN

The family watched the river for ten or fifteen minutes, looking for more wildlife. Finally Dad stood up and brushed off his pants. "Well, do you think it might be time for us to head back?" he asked.

Mom pointed to the water. "Not yet!" she replied. "There's a beaver across the way."

The beaver was swimming in the river, leaving a little V in its wake. It lumbered out of the water and slowly waddled up the riverbank.

"Hey!" Morgan exclaimed. "There are two more!" One of the beavers was swimming near a hole at the river's edge. "That might be its lodge," she said. The other beaver was in the water.

The beavers continued swimming along, crawling up the bank and, at times, disappearing into their den. The Parkers stood watching for several satisfying minutes.

Then Morgan saw another animal. "Look!" she called out.

The animal reached the slope adjacent to the water and slid as if on its own personal waterslide down the grassy embankment and slipped into the water.

"It's an otter!" Mom exclaimed.

Once in the water, the otter floated on its back for a while. Suddenly the otter began performing a series of rolls and somersaults close to the surface of the water, like a gymnast, then swam upstream.

"Quite a little show we're getting," Dad said.

Just then another bird glided through the calm water. "Look," James said, pointing upstream. It was a striking bird, beautifully black and white with a reddish orange bill.

The amateur Parker birding family thought it could be some sort of duck, then shifted their position to "grebe" and then to "loon."

There was a troop of birders close to the water. One of them put down his giant binoculars and gave the Parkers the scoop. "It's a male merganser."

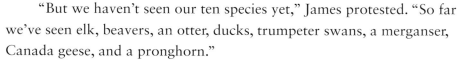

"Really?" Mom asked. "Shows you just how much we know."

It was close to 9:00 p.m. and getting dark when Dad said again, "Should we all head back?"

"But we haven't seen our ten species yet," James protested. "So far we've seen elk, beavers, an otter, ducks, trumpeter swans, a merganser, Canada geese, and a pronghorn."

"That makes eight," Morgan announced.

Dad slapped at a mosquito trying to drill into his arm. "Are we counting bugs, too?"

The Parkers all laughed and then walked back to the car, deciding eight out of ten was still pretty darn good.

The Black Marmot

"It's my turn now to tell what happened next in the Tetons," James announced. "Can I have the tape recorder, please?" he asked Dad.

"Sure, here you go, James," Dad replied, handing it back to James. James started:

We met a ranger, Kari, and a group of others at the flagpole outside the Jenny Lake Visitor Center. From there we followed the moose tracks painted on the cement walkway to our boat taxi. I noticed a sign at the boat dock listing animals sighted and the dates they were most recently seen. Black bear, eagle, and moose were among those on the list. I wondered what we were going to spot.

"I wonder if we'll see a bear," Morgan said as she stepped onto the gently swaying boat and sat next to James.

"Maybe a cub," James responded.

"A grizzly cub!" Morgan replied.

Mom and Dad sat behind the twins. Mom leaned forward, "As long as it's from a distance."

After crossing the lake and unloading on the dock of the western shore, Ranger Kari began leading the group on the popular trail up toward Hidden Falls.

Soon Kari stopped everyone near a rushing stream and said, "In 1874 Ferdinand Hayden led an expedition to this area to explore and document features of the West. Many men accompanied him, including a man named Richard Leigh. Leigh's wife, Jenny, is who Jenny Lake is named for, and just north of Jenny Lake is Leigh Lake."

Kari continued, "There are rocks in the Tetons that are some of the oldest in all of North America—up to 2.7 billion years old. But the Tetons are actually very young mountains, at least in geologic time. They haven't been worn down yet, and that is why they are so spiked and rugged."

"I guess we're *really* young, huh?" Morgan whispered to James.

Kari explained more about the mountains. "The Tetons were first carved by rivers creating V-shaped canyons. Later the mountains and canyons were chiseled away by massive glaciers, making for the U-shaped canyons that are seen in some areas today. The glaciers in the park used to be thousands of feet thick. Now only a half dozen or so remain from the Little Ice Age of ten thousand to fourteen thousand years ago, but they are melting rapidly. Soon, all of the glaciers will be gone, so the rivers will be carving just V-shaped canyons again."

James whispered to Morgan, "If we could come back in about a million years, we could see all the changes. Wouldn't that be neat?"

As the group proceeded to a rocky area, Kari invited everyone to sit down. She handed out pictures of the different types of rocks found in the Tetons. "Some of the more dominant rocks—metamorphic and granite—are highly erosion resistant, and they change very slowly. In fact, Mount Moran is considered the 'mother of all rocks' because it has all the different kinds of Teton rocks in it, including a little bit of sandstone."

Kari went on to give more information about the geologic makeup of the mountains, and then the group continued on its way.

Soon they approached an area of steeply sloped boulders. A blur of golden fur dashed across the trail in front of them. The animal quickly scampered into a crevasse between some rocks.

There were three or four more similar animals scattered among the boulders. "Those are marmots," Kari said. "They are part of a colony of ten to twenty." One of the marmots was lying flat on a rock, sunbathing. Another stood straight up and while it did, it let out a shrieking, piercing, whistle-like sound that startled everyone.

"That was sure loud!" Morgan exclaimed.

Then a completely black critter skittered down the rocks and into a hole.

"What was that?" James asked.

"That was also a marmot," Kari replied. "Teton marmots can sometimes be black, and that's fairly unique. The Tetons may be one of the few places in the world where this happens."

"Pretty cool!" Mom replied.

Soon they all made it to one of the two major destinations along the trail, Hidden Falls. Everyone stood at the fenced-in viewing area and gazed at the waterfall with the large cliffs nearby. Hidden Falls plunged down. It was quite a torrent.

Morgan interrupted James's story, but spoke loud enough to be recorded. "Remember, Kari told us that Hidden Falls isn't really a waterfall."

"Right, because it's not actually free-falling but cascading," James replied.

"Still, it was a most beautiful sight," Mom added.
Then James continued . . .

The group crossed a few footbridges and began hiking the final switch-backs up to Inspiration Point. Kari stopped and pointed toward the mountains. "Native Americans called this area 'Teewinot,' meaning many peaks. We can see Teewinot Mountain up there—with several jagged peaks on it. To the far right," she pointed, "is Mount Owen, still with lots of snow on it. And the one in the middle is the tallest mountain in the range, Grand Teton, at 13,770 feet."

As the hikers traveled farther up, a family approached them on their way down. Morgan, James, Mom, and Dad had to move out of the way to give them some room on the narrow, rocky path. The dad had a young child in a carrier on his back. The girl kissed her father's shoulders and said, "That's because you are doing such a great job hiking on this rocky trail, Daddy!"

"I remember those days," Mom said, smiling.

Finally they reached Inspiration Point, elevation 7,200 feet. Kari continued sharing, "The earth's plates in the area have been colliding for ten million years or so. This leads to earthquakes, causing the Teton mountains to rise quickly while the valley is sinking even faster. For every foot the mountains have risen, the valley has sunk four times more. But the mountains are definitely growing."

James leaned over to Morgan, "So, when we come back in a million years to check the shape of the valleys, we can also see how much taller the peaks are!"

From the vantage point looking out over the lake, the group learned that there used to be cabins, rodeos, and billboards along the lake and in the valley until the mountains became a national park in 1929 and Jackson Hole was added in 1950.

"I much prefer how we see it now," Mom said.

Kari concluded the guided hike, and most of the group hung out for the views and to ask some questions. As Morgan snapped a picture overlooking Jenny Lake, a group of hikers strutted down from Cascade Canyon. One stopped when he saw the ranger.

"There's a moose and a calf up the canyon," he informed her.

That got the Parkers interest. Dad asked, "How far up?"

"Probably a mile, maybe less."

The Parkers all looked at each other and nodded when Kari said, "It's a beautiful hike anyway and our most popular trail into the mountains."

And with that, Morgan, James, Mom, and Dad were off again for more hiking.

James turned off the recorder and looked at everyone in the car. "I think I got it all, right?"

Morgan, Mom, and Dad agreed.

Is There an Animal Outside of Your Thumb?

"I think this is a good spot for you to take over," James said as he passed Morgan the recorder.

"I remember that moose so well, and there are a ton of pictures to show for it," Morgan said. "So here goes."

Morgan, James, Mom, and Dad left Inspiration Point—and the large crowds of people—behind and began hiking up Cascade Canyon. As the trail climbed, Mom said, "It feels like a little training hike for the bigger things to come."

"We're hiking right underneath the Tetons' tallest spiked peaks," Dad added. "From this angle they have sort of a Matterhorn shape."

The trail climbed through a rocky area but soon leveled out. The Parkers noticed a group of people ahead staring into a marshy area, and picked up their pace.

The family joined a dozen or so other wildlife watchers and saw the two moose right away. It was the mom and calf that they had heard about. They were both lying in the grass with their heads perked up as if on alert.

Morgan held out her thumb in line, first with the adult moose and then the calf. "I think we're just about at the right distance away," she reported. "I can't see either moose outside of my thumb."

Mom looked at Morgan. "Where did you learn that technique?"

"From a pamphlet at the lodge," Morgan replied.

The family watched the moose for some time while Morgan took pictures. Then they decided to take the long way back to their car, the trail along the north shore of Jenny Lake.

James looked over a map of the area. "It's about five miles back to the visitor center," he announced.

The Parkers took off downhill and soon turned north at the trail junction. Now it seemed that they had the trail, and the forest, all to themselves.

As Morgan, James, Mom, and Dad snaked downhill, they almost immediately heard a distinctive snapping of bushes. Instantly the whole clan was on full alert. Mom grabbed James's arm and Dad took Morgan's. With their free hands, both Mom and Dad took their bear spray canisters off of their belts.

There was more snapping, but no one could identify the source of the sound. "There's something big in there," Mom whispered.

The Parkers took several slow, cautious steps down the trail.

Suddenly Mom gasped. "It's a bull moose!"

The Parkers all froze in their tracks. The massive mammal was about thirty feet off the trail. It was yanking leaves with its mouth off a willow tree, one powerful, thrusting pull after another.

"It sure seems hungry," Morgan whispered as she pulled out her camera and started taking pictures.

The moose paused for a brief second and glanced at the Parkers.

"Oops," Mom said.

But the moose went back to eating. That's when Morgan realized, "We're much closer than we should be. I don't even have to hold up my thumb."

The family looked at each other, then skedaddled out of there until the animal was far from sight.

As soon as the Parkers felt safe again, they stopped and took what seemed like their first breath in several minutes. Then everyone started blurting out details of the encounter . . .

"I first heard you gasp, Mom."

"It was so big and we were so close!"

"It was just ripping off leaves from that tree."

"I couldn't take my eyes off of it!"

Finally Mom said, "I know it was close to the trail and we couldn't help being where we were. But moose are highly unpredictable and potentially very dangerous. We had to move on."

"Still," Dad admitted, "that was a once in a lifetime."

Soon the trail broke out of the forest and into sunshine. Morgan, James, Mom, and Dad slowed their pace and circled Jenny Lake, crossing a bridge over a rushing stream along the way. On the eastern shore they passed several picnic areas. The family stopped at one and enjoyed a lunch of crackers, peanut butter, and apples.

"What a day!" Morgan said.

Big Plans for Little People

"Is it OK if I tell this story?" James asked. "Because I was the one who met the Scouts first when we got to Colter Bay."

"I grant you first right," Morgan replied, but then added, "However, my memory tells me we met Greg and Cameron at the same time."

"Maybe so," James said. "But, still, can I tell it?"

When no one said "no," James took the recorder and began.

The Parkers left Lizard Creek Campground, a one-night stay at the northern end of Jackson Lake, and again checked into the rustic and quaint Colter Bay cabins. "These kind of remind me of the Lincoln Logs we used to construct in our living room," James said to Morgan.

The Parkers were in a fourplex unit. Each unit had two twin beds, so Dad and James stayed in one and Mom and Morgan stayed in another room across the way. There were men's and women's bathrooms down the hall.

As Morgan, James, Mom, and Dad were unloading all of their gear from the car into the rooms, another car pulled up. Two men and two teenagers also began unpacking their gear and spreading it out on a bench nearby. The Parkers watched them with intrigue, noticing supplies similar to their own: water bottles, a tiny camp stove, water filters, bear canisters, first-aid kits, freeze-dried foods, hats, sunscreen, packs, tents, mattress pads, and so on. The two teenagers also had Scout logos on their shirts.

"They sure have some nice equipment," Dad said while he hauled in his old and tattered backpack. "My pack here has far too many miles on it."

The two Scouts heard Dad's comment. They looked over and acknowledged the Parkers, and also appeared to glance at Dad's well-worn pack, but then they kept on talking to each other.

After a while the two Scouts and the adults with them took a topo map of the Tetons over to the hood of their car and began discussing details. James tried his best to nonchalantly eavesdrop on their conversation as he walked between the family car and the room with supplies in hand, but he didn't hear much.

Soon Mom said, "OK. I think that's enough unpacking for now. Why don't we walk over to the restaurant and get dinner."

After a quick meal at the John Colter Cafe, Morgan, James, Mom, and Dad took a stroll along the Lakeshore Trail, past the marina.

Several other families were also walking along the casual pathway. A pair of geese with fluffy little goslings lapped along the shore with the tiny waves.

"They're so cute," Morgan mentioned while snapping a photo.

The short walk led the family to a peninsula overlooking part of Jackson Lake. Others were already out there fishing, or just gazing at the lake and the Teton skyline beyond. It was a picturesque sight.

Morgan turned back to look at the baby geese, then all of the sudden elbowed James. "The Scouts are here!" she exclaimed.

James looked over and saw them, perched on a log and gazing at the snowcapped peaks. He meandered closer, still curious, and began listening.

"Tomorrow we head out on the Teton Crest Trail," one said.

"The number-one-rated backpack in all of North America," the other replied.

Now James was sucked in because that's exactly where the Parkers were going.

James walked closer, and with Morgan at his side, he joined in. "We're going up there, too."

The soon-to-be-backpackers looked up. "Hey it's our cabin buddies!" one said as a greeting.

James introduced himself and Morgan.

"I'm Cameron," the younger-looking Scout said, "and this is my brother Greg. Our Uncle Richard and his friend, Jeff, are back at the cabin. We're starting the Teton Crest Trail tomorrow."

"We're heading up there, too," James repeated. "But not until the day after tomorrow."

"We're rock climbing tomorrow," Morgan added.

"Where are you all from?" Cameron asked.

Upon hearing those words, Mom and Dad waltzed over.

"San Luis Obispo, California," Morgan responded. "How about you?"

"We're from Georgia, so we're not used to these mountains. But, really, how could anyone be?"

Dad popped a question. "Are you going up the ski lift?"

"Yep, and coming out at Leigh Lake."

"Just like us," James realized out loud. "Maybe we'll see you along the trail."

"Maybe," Greg chimed in. "But we're leaving tomorrow."

"How long are you taking to hike the whole thing?" Mom asked.

"Five days," Cameron replied. "To cover the thirty-nine miles. The first day we're going slow to get acclimated. But we're also planning a layover day, or maybe a day hike toward Static Peak."

"Maybe we *will* see you along the trail, then," James said. "We're hoping to do the whole thing in four or five days, depending on how it goes."

Cameron gave James a double take. Then, after pondering for a few

seconds, he said, "Those are some big plans for little people!"

James smiled, feeling confident of their itinerary, at least at the moment.

The six fell silent for a bit, again gazing at the incredible, lofty peaks. Then, after some time, Mom said, "I love these slow sunsets. But we do have a big day planned tomorrow, so we best head in."

The Parkers said good-bye to the Scouts. As they were walking away, James called out, "I really do hope to see you in a few days!"

Greg and Cameron smiled and gave the family a thumbs-up.

Think of the Stick-Man

The family was now about an hour east of Reno and driving west. James was reading, Mom was doing a crossword, and it was Dad's turn to drive. Morgan looked at her relaxed, contemplative family and called out, "I think I'll tape what happened when we rock climbed."

"OK," Mom replied. "That was such an important part of our Teton experience."

Morgan picked up the recorder.

The Parkers met two Exum guides at their office near the Jenny Lake Visitor Center. The guides, Brendon and Andy, got all their gear set and had each family member find suitable shoes and helmets. They all walked over to the Jenny Lake boat dock and boarded the ferry across the lake.

When they got to the landing on the other side, Andy took Mom and Dad one way to begin their training for scaling Grand Teton. Brendon took James and Morgan nearby to go climbing for the day. But, as it turned out, they were doing many of the same things in the same area.

Morgan, James, and Brendon headed up the Hidden Falls Trail, where the Parkers had just been the day before. Soon they slipped under a fence and went off-trail, up a long, sloping granite slab.

Brendon instructed, "Keep your nose over your toes and take small steps. Keep your feet pointed forward and don't lean back, or you could lose your balance."

Brendon demonstrated the techniques, then he climbed back down to James and Morgan and said, "OK, who's first?"

Morgan volunteered by stepping forward.

As she placed one foot after another up the granite slope, James called out below. "Great job, Morgan, you're a natural!"

Brendon followed Morgan all the way to the top of the slab, then shared some techniques for going downhill. "Do the same thing, nose over toes, small steps, and feet forward."

Soon Morgan made it halfway back to James. "Wait here," the Exum guide said.

Morgan sat down and watched Brendon guide James up the same slope. James joined his sister a few minutes later with a big smile and said, "These sticky rubber shoes are like miracle grips."

Now Brendon showed Morgan and James a "boulder problem." "Helmets first!" he ordered.

The helmeted twins scrambled up a few boulders with Brendon spotting them, or protecting their fall, each time from below. He also showed the kids how to "chimney" by pushing their feet against one wall of the rock and their backside against the other, then working their way up. Brendon called this "using oppositional weight."

While James chimneyed, Morgan searched for her parents and wondered how they were doing, but couldn't see them.

Brendon read Morgan's mind. "We'll all be meeting soon," he said.

On the next boulder, Brendon demonstrated how to use fingers for holds. While the guide spotted, James and Morgan began a little game. "This time you can only use two fingers on each hand," Morgan announced.

After James's turn, he came scrambling back while grinning and said, "One finger this time!"

Morgan tried to abide by the latest rule, but at one point her grip was so tentative that she had to grab on with a full hand to prevent herself

THE FIRST ONES UP THE MOUNTAIN

In 1929 Glenn Exum, at age sixteen, began climbing in the Teton Range with Paul Petzoldt. Two years later Glenn scaled a never-climbed-before route on the Grand Teton. Alone, Glenn had no rope and had borrowed leather-cleated shoes that were two sizes too big for him. He managed to ascend an area on the mountain called "Wall Street" where he had to walk back and forth along the ledge numerous times before finding necessary handholds. He eventually jumped across to make the ridge toward the summit. He scaled the pitches on the ridge and summited the now-named Exum Ridge, the most popular way up the Grand Teton.

Later, Glenn advocated that mountain guides should give their clients as much of the climbing experience as possible. This meant learning knots, rope handling, and rappelling, as well as safety hazards and how to treat the sensitive mountain environment. Now all who use Exum Mountain Guides services get the full experience of climbing or summiting whichever mountain they choose to ascend for adventure. Exum guides have shepherded over fifty thousand people to the summit of the Grand Teton at 13,770 feet.

from falling. After that she sort of returned to the one-finger technique, then said from above, "Oh well, at least I tried, and I got up here."

Brendon said, "The more techniques you have available to you, and the more you trust them, the better you climb."

At the top of the slab, Brendon showed the twins how to "mantle," or push up, like when getting out of a swimming pool.

"There are a lot of things about rock climbing to learn," Brendon said, "like under-clings, side-holds, finger-jams, and hand-jams." He demonstrated each on the rock with his fingers and hands.

"Now," Brendon said, "I want you to each use at least three techniques that we've worked on going up this rock."

James tried the first time up to vary his approach, but it seemed to him like he was just getting up the rock any way he could. The second time, though, he used a hand-jam, and grabbed a side-hold, before mantling over the boulder.

"Wow! Excellent. You are well on your way to being a mountaineer," the guide said.

As the twins continued to work on technique, all seemed to be going quite well until James slipped on a hold and his knee and shoulder thumped against the rock.

Brendon reacted quickly to stop his fall, but James had already stopped himself. "Are you OK?" Brendon asked.

"Yes," James said, but he wasn't sure. He yanked his way to the top before grimacing a bit and shaking out his shoulder.

After a moment for rest and water, Brendon next led the twins to another chimney section. There Brendon taught Morgan and James bridging, or stemming. "Put one foot on each side of the corner," he said.

James went first and Brendon said to him, "Make sure you have a good hold at each foothold. And I'll be right below you, spotting."

James placed his feet on opposite sides and grabbed above with his hands. He hoisted himself up. After that, it was a few easy moves to the top.

Once he came back down, it was Morgan's turn. She got stuck after the first move up the rock. She held there for a minute, looking up and around, trying to figure out what to do next.

Brendon decided to help and said, "I like the way you are trying to figure things out. But what if you try this?" he pointed. "Put your foot over here, and your hand in this spot."

Once Morgan managed the maneuver, Brendon said, "There you go. Now look up. Do you see any holds up there?"

Morgan studied the rock, hesitatingly, and even started to shake.

"Don't worry, I've got you," Brendon said. Then he added, "See if you can get your foot over here."

Morgan worked out the suggestion, then passed onto another move. "Excellent," Brendon said. "There are many different ways to do this."

"What about over here?" Morgan asked.

Brendon replied, "You can do it. Trust your instincts. And know that I have you spotted no matter what."

Morgan lunged for the hold and grabbed it. But it was a long reach, so her feet swung out and dangled like a pendulum back and forth. After a few panicked seconds of hanging on one arm, she managed to find a place for her feet to barely step onto.

"Whoo-hoo! What a move. Way to go!" Brendon exclaimed.

That response made Morgan smile.

From there the crux move was complete. Morgan scrambled quickly to the top and climbed down to high fives and praise from both James and Brendon. The guide said, "That was quite a flair for the dramatic, Morgan, hanging up there like that. But you also demonstrated perfect perseverance. You didn't give up!"

"Thanks for the tips along the way," Morgan replied.

They moved on. "This crack is the 'grand finale' of our morning," Brendon said.

James and Morgan tried different techniques and routes up the crack. They were putting their whole morning together at this last place before the "real" climbing started. At one point after Morgan climbed around and down, James said, "You looked like Spider-Woman up there."

"It's the shoes," Morgan said. "It's like they have magic grips on them."

Brendon informed them, "No, it's you, but the shoes do help. They're approach shoes. They're for a combination of hiking and climbing. And we're doing both today, really."

Morgan and James spent a few more minutes crack-climbing then moved on, soon ducking under the fence at the crowded Hidden Falls area. They scrambled up some boulders and made it to the basic slab area. That's when James and Morgan realized they weren't the only ones learning to climb today. There were Exum groups all around the slab. And Mom and Dad were already up at the top!

Brendon found a little stick and held it upright against the rock. "Let's call this Stick-Man," he said. "If Stick-Man clings to the granite," Brendon showed the stick going up the granite boulder, "and hangs on with his upper part too closely, his feet will go out from under him and he'll slip down."

Brendon then showed the stick figure with the top of it right next to the sloping boulder and the bottom slipping out. "The trick is to stay vertical and upright. Your feet will grip much better that way. And remember to use any of the techniques you think are necessary."

After the twins harnessed up, Brendon taught James and Morgan how to tie in. They each made a figure eight on a rope, looped it through two places in their harness, then traced the figure back by following through so it was all doubled up.

Once James and Morgan were secure, the guide explained what was going to happen. "I now have both of you on rope. We're going to climb the Basic Slab in five pitches, all the way to that Douglas fir up there. But first I'll climb up to that ledge."

Brendon expertly moved up to the ledge. After fixing some ropes, he looked down at James and Morgan. "OK, who's first?"

James jumped up, "Me!"

"OK," Brendon said. "Wait until I pull all the rope, though."

"Don't forget about Stick-Man, James!" Morgan reminded him.

As Brendon pulled up the excess slack in the lifeline, he said, "Yes, Stick-Man is one way to look at it. But here's another: Keep your hips high and your heels low. The more you lean your upper body into the rock, the greater the chance of slipping."

Once the rope was ready, James scaled the first section like a mountaineer. When he got to Brendon, the guide anchored him in.

"Can I go?" Morgan looked up, excited.

"Wait until the rope is ready," Brendon replied calmly.

When the rope was taut, she began climbing on some glacial polish. "Press your heels down," Brendon said.

That did the trick. In not much more than an instant, Morgan was right next to James, ready to begin round two.

Morgan and James soon made it up the next four pitches, where they were met by Mom and Dad.

"Nice climbing, you two," Dad said. "We were watching you. You sure you don't want to scale the Grand with us?" Dad joked.

James and Morgan smiled, knowing that actually *could be* part of their itinerary, but not for a few years.

Mom held out sack lunches, and Morgan and James dove in.

The Big Drop

After lunch, it was back to more climbing for the Parkers. James and Morgan returned to the Basic Slab and worked on new routes while each got better with technique.

Mom and Dad went on to scale "Open Book," a two-pitch, 5.7-rated climb. . . .

Morgan stopped recording. "I think I'll pass the story on to the two of you now," she said to Mom and Dad. "This is your part to tell."

She then handed the recorder to Dad, who turned it on and began: "At first my heart was thumping. But I tried, and sometimes was able, to get myself to relax. I got better at this as time went on. I also learned to trust that one way or another, I was going to get up there."

Mom chimed in: "It was challenging having to clean up the gear while following Andy. At one point I couldn't get a cam out. It was wedged in there pretty good. And just taking my hands off the rock to work on it was a struggle. It felt like I was going to fall. My heart started racing every time I tried to free the cam. I even called up to him at one point, 'I can't get this thing out!' Eventually I had to unclip from my belt a little clean-up tool to help wiggle the gear free. I mean, I had no choice. You can't go past the gear placed in the rock."

"But it was like getting a little reward every time I took one of those out and clipped it in," Dad said.

"Once we got to the top," Mom went on, "Andy short-roped us down. It was like being on a little leash in case we fell. And we worked our way back to the base."

"Right around then," Dad interjected, "we saw the two of you rappelling off of a cliff!"

"It was amazing, and a little nerve-wracking, to see you spider-walking down a rope, all the way to the ground. You both looked so good at it!" Mom said.

"Brendon was with us the whole way," James said.

"I do have to admit, as smooth as it looked, I breathed a little easier once I saw your feet touch ground," Mom replied.

"Then it was our turn," Dad said. "We did our rappel off an over-hang above and around 'Open Book,' which was a 150-foot drop."

"That," Mom exclaimed, "made my heart drop into my gut!"

"Here's how I remember it," Dad said. "Andy had me anchored in above the rappel. We set our bowline knot, and he also had me double-backed. I could pass out on the rope, he said, and he would still be able to lower me safely. Andy then had me back up a foot or so, heading backward toward the big drop. 'Go ahead, lean back,' he said. 'I've got you. You aren't going anywhere.' But I didn't want to go. I mean, it isn't natural to lean backward over a 150-foot drop. I certainly was scared."

"Actually," Mom interjected, "I think you were freaking out."

Dad smiled. "Yeah, I imagine that was what it looked like. But I slowly inched backward until I was right at the edge of the cliff. I got more of a sense, then, that soon there was going to be nothing but air below me. 'Go ahead,' Andy said again while I hung out backward, close to the edge. So I inched back as slowly as I could go."

"That's about when we saw you," James said.

"Well," Dad said, "I've never started a backpack from a ski lift before. That was a first. But there we were, walking on the barren mountaintop ski runs with a few snow patches here and there until we found our trail."

"And it was soon after that we got our first look at the incredible wildflowers that accompanied us pretty much on the whole journey," Mom continued. "They were amazing. I only knew the names of a few of them. Moss campion, forget-me-nots, and sky pilots come to mind now, but there were far too many to remember."

"So many colors and types," Dad added.

"I remember you saying it was mind-boggling, Mom," Morgan said.

Mom went on. "Every time we turned a corner, they got better and better. More colorful, denser, and with more variety. I kept asking you to take pictures."

"Don't worry, I took plenty," Morgan said.

"I realized," Mom continued, "that the higher elevations of the Tetons are a different world than down below. It was like spring up there, whereas the Jackson Hole Valley was bathed-in-summer dry."

"Remember that I said the hills looked like clumps of Fruit Loops?" James asked.

"I do remember that," Mom replied. "And it wasn't just their appearance. It was their fragrance, the aroma, and we kept walking on the path right through them."

"What a difference a few thousand feet in elevation can make," Dad added.

"We were in the alpine tundra world," Mom said. "But the last few miles on that first day, I remember, had so many ups and downs. We were all very tired."

"Finally we made it to Marion Lake," Dad interjected, *"nestled in a deep mountain bowl with huge cliffs behind it. Our campsite was a good deal away from the lake. But we kept going back to filter water, look at the scenery, or try and swim."*

"Try is the right word," Mom said. *"I recall I only got up to my ankles. The water was so cold."*

"Remember the three bull moose we saw across the canyon after dinner?" James asked.

"Then a deer and two fawns came right into our campsite. They got so close," Morgan added.

"Really," Mom concluded, *"it was a perfect day."*

Marion Lake

The Echo

As the Parkers continued on their journey home, James jumped right in to begin to describe their second day on the Teton Crest Trail. "I was woken at the crack of dawn by a bunch of racket outside our tent."

"We thought it was a bear," Morgan said.

"Turned out it was that deer and her fawns," James replied.

"I had already grabbed the bear spray," Dad added, "just in case."

James went on. "As we hiked in the morning of our second day, Dad, you looked at the Tetons looming ahead and said, 'They look like a Shangri-la.'"

"The more we saw of those mountains, the more astonishing and exotic they seemed," Mom added.

"I know I felt a little stronger hiking that second morning. I guess I was getting used to the altitude," James continued.

"That's really because your pack weighed a lot less because of all the food you ate the night before," Morgan added with a playful laugh.

James smiled. "We were also helping to train you, Mom and Dad, for climbing the Grand Teton by doing this backpack."

Mom replied, "I can't think of any better way to get in shape for summiting the Grand than by hauling a full backpack at those elevations for five days."

"I hope the recorder is picking up everyone's voices," James added. *"Anyway, at one point we could see the plains and valleys of Idaho all the way down the mountains to our left. And then somewhere along the trail, we saw what we thought was wolf scat."*

Morgan looked down at a pile of poop next to the trail. "It has fur in it!"

Mom, Dad, and James also stopped to inspect the scat. "I bet that's from a wolf," Mom said. "It's pretty big."

The family scanned the horizon, looking for a large carnivore, but there was none to be seen. They hiked on and made it to Death Canyon Shelf.

As they walked along, a moose and her calf were nibbling on some small plants right near a backpacker campsite, by the trail. The Parkers watched the animals as they walked by. "Good thing we didn't camp there last night," James said.

"I agree," Mom said. "But look at the scenery here! Death Canyon Shelf, what a unique area. That cliff above us is huge, and the valley below is so far down. We're right in the middle of the two."

As the Parkers hiked through Death Canyon Shelf, they suddenly heard "Hello!" called out from down the trail. "Hello," the voice bounced off the mountains and then faded in a circle of echoes.

Morgan, James, Mom, and Dad looked at each other with excited, childlike, beaming faces.

Then James yelled as loud as he could, "Moose!"

"Moose" bounced off the walls of the mountains.

"Bear!" Morgan now tried.

"Bear" circulated among the high peaks and valleys where the Parkers were.

"We're just joking. There's no animals," Mom called out.

"We're just joking . . ." echoed off the cliffs.

Dad yelled, "Marmot!"

"Marmot . . . marmot . . . marmot . . ." the call slowly faded away.

Finally Mom tried, "Hello!"

"Hello" echoed off the high mountain walls clearly several more times than any other word attempted so far.

James did one more. "Wolf!"

"Wolf . . . wolf . . . wolf . . ."

"You know," Dad said, "people might think we actually see some of those animals near us and be on high alert."

"'Hello' worked best anyway," Morgan concluded. "It ricocheted at least five times."

Then someone down the trail shouted "Hello!" back.

Again the Parkers were drawn in. They answered the call with the four of them shouting "Hello!" as loud as they could, all at once.

And the unseen group answered with a "Hello" of their own! The Parkers all cracked up.

James said, "That was fun!"

"Still, we do have some hiking to do," Mom added, ending the echo game.

"And I think we'd better go quickly," Dad said, looking at the sky. "The clouds are building up."

Eventually the family huffed up the last hill of the day. They tried to keep their pace brisk as the sky continued to become more ominous, but the high elevation and steep climb kept the Parkers moving slowly.

Finally the family made it to Sunset Lake. They scrambled to get their tent set up and had just pounded the last stake in place when the storm broke loose.

Dad paused a moment to gather his thoughts. With all the events coming up, he didn't want to leave anything out, or tell it in the wrong order. "We started down after the high point on the pass. That's when the views really kicked in."

"Boy, did they ever," Mom added. "Like the Grand Teton way above us. It had a cloud billowing off the peak like a plume of smoke. It must have been really windy up there that morning!"

"It was pretty amazing to see it that close," Dad said. "But we also were very close to another Teton high-country spectacle. A few switchbacks down and we were staring eye level at the small, but clearly glacial, Schoolroom Glacier."

"Why is it called 'School-room'?" James asked.

"Because it's a good place to learn the parts of a glacier," Dad replied. "A glacier

Moraine

Glacial lake

Glacier

Bergschrund

has bergschrunds, *or cracks, in it from the movement in the ice. It also had a perfectly shaped circular moraine at its base from the glacier slowly plowing down rock debris over time."*

"We went up to it later," James said.

"We had to," Dad said, "even though it was off the main trail. But remember the awesome turquoise color of the lake below? That means the glacier is grinding the rock underneath it into a flour. And when that stuff gets into water below, it makes the lake or stream look silty and turquoise."

The details everyone had been anticipating finally came next.

"We kept winding our way down the switchbacks with better and better views of the glacier along the way," Dad recalled. *"It was almost as if you could reach out and touch it. But then we saw the two backpacks ditched by the side trail to the glacier."*

"We recognized Greg and Cameron's equipment right away," James said, *"The packs were taller than ours and grayish green."*

"I remember when we saw their packs, I looked over toward the glacier, hoping to see Greg and Cameron," Mom said. *"But I think they were behind the rock outcropping."*

James added, *"I was excited, like we were about to meet up again with some old friends and we could share trail stories. But little did we know . . ."*

"So we kept heading down the switchbacks," Dad continued. *"And that's when we heard the screams. And someone shouting, 'Greg! Greg!'"*

"It was frightening, no, spine chilling," Morgan interjected. "And then it was quiet, eerily quiet, for several seconds."

"Soon we heard another long, spine-tingling scream from someone who was definitely hurt, followed by what sounded like rocks tumbling and cracking, and then it all stopped," James said. "I don't think we'll ever forget that moment."

"By then we were well below the side trail to the glacier," Dad said. "We looked up toward the ice, but the moraine blocked our view. We couldn't see much at all."

"I know my heart sank," Mom added. "I knew Greg or Cameron, or both, were in trouble, but I didn't know immediately what to do."

"My first thought was to run up there," Dad said. "Then I remembered something about the moraine. From above we could see an outlet stream splitting it down the middle. I thought we might find out more of what was going on, or even get to them easier, if we went to that stream. A few more switchbacks down and there we were, right next to the silty, milky meltwater below the lake and glacier."

"And there was a trail through that part of the moraine that led right to the lake!" James recalled. "So we hurried on up."

Greg and Cameron— An Interlude

Greg and Cameron ditched their packs at the side trail to the glacier. "Let's go check it out!" Greg beamed to his younger brother.

The faint but distinct path led straight to the ice and snow. Soon the two Scouts were right up on it. But it was still early season in the high country, and some additional snow from the previous winter clung to the fringes of the permanent ice field.

Greg and Cameron left the path and stepped onto the ice. Greg led the way, shuffling his feet to make distinct, flatter steps for Cameron to use and for them both to follow on their way off the glacier later.

A few dozen feet or so out onto the small glacier, Greg turned toward Cameron. "Did you hear that?" he smiled. "Somewhere in the glacier there is creaking or groaning."

"Maybe the ice is trying to tell us something," Cameron said. "It's kind of spooky."

Cameron peered around the steep, precarious sheet of ice. Then he turned cautiously toward Greg. "Maybe we should get off the glacier and find Richard and Jeff. And they can come explore out here with us."

"You're right," Greg replied. "Let's get off the ice."

Greg gingerly turned to step back, but the snow instantly gave out underneath him. His foot broke through a weak spot, causing him to lose his balance and tumble down the mountain. "Ahh! . . . Help!" he screamed as he shot down the steep snow.

Cameron watched in horror as Greg plummeted down the mountain. About a hundred feet below, Greg's weight collapsed a side-clinging snowfield, and he crashed inside what instantly became an ice cave.

Greg had completely disappeared from Cameron's view. "Greg!" he called, panicking. "Greg!" The screams filled the silence that had surrounded the glacier only moments before and carried out to the glacial lake below.

Just then the Parkers arrived. They looked up and saw Cameron halfway up the glacier, just off the rocks. Even though he was far away, the boy's voice and demeanor personified panic and pure horror.

From their vantage point, the Parkers could see the newly formed ice cave. They could also see a leg protruding from the jumble of rocks, snow, and ice inside. "Greg's in there!" Dad cried out. Then he cupped his hands and shouted up to Cameron, "He's in there!"

Cameron called back to the Parkers. "Is he OK? Can you get to him?"

Mom, Dad, James, and Morgan quickly assessed the situation from the turquoise body of water where they were now standing. The lake was too deep and silty to see the bottom, and the moraine was large and steep and full of loose rock. There were no visible trails to the other side of the lake, where a large chunk of ice dangled into the water.

"We can't get to him from here," Dad called up.

Then Dad turned to Morgan, James, and Mom. "I can't stand here and watch. I have to go up there. Stay here and watch the glacier for any unseen hazards, then shout them up. OK?"

"Be careful," Mom replied.

Mom found her cell phone and immediately dialed 911. Once she got an answer, she hurriedly explained the emergency and where it was.

Dad ran back to the main trail. He quickly found the family's first-aid kit in his pack and took off uphill to where Cameron was. It was slow going, though, as at nearly ten thousand feet, it was hard to run.

Cameron, meanwhile, stood up and quickly reviewed his options. He jumped off the snow and ran back to his pack. Morgan, James, and Mom saw him take a pouch out of one of his compartments then dash back to the glacier, using the steps Greg had made earlier, to walk carefully yet quickly toward his brother.

Cameron took some rope from the pouch and, holding one end, threw the rest of the pouch down toward the collapsed area of snow where Greg had disappeared. He then secured the remaining rope around some boulders just off the glacier. He tested the rope quickly, making sure it could hold his weight. Then Cameron wrapped the rope around his waist and grabbed it, and began to lower himself down to the ice cave.

Mom called up as loud as she could. "My husband is coming!"

Cameron called back. "I have to get down there now. That's my brother!"

Just then two hikers came running up to the Parkers. Mom recognized them right away. It was Richard and Jeff, who they had met with Greg and Cameron at Colter Bay.

"What happened?" Richard said while trying to catch his breath.

Mom pointed to the glacier. "We didn't see it, but it appears that Greg's down there and is definitely hurt."

Richard and Jeff quickly looked around and realized they, too, couldn't get to Greg from where they were. Just then Dad appeared far above. He was approaching where Cameron had tied in.

"That's my husband," Mom reported.

"Let's get up there, too," Richard said to Jeff while watching Cameron's attempt to rappel his way to Greg.

As they took off, Mom called out, "I called 911 and backcountry rangers are on their way."

Richard waved and shouted back. "Gotcha!"

"I'm so relieved they are here," Mom said, looking at the experts trained for just such an event. Dad said something to the group above, then took off down the trail to rejoin his family.

One of the rangers weaved his rope between his legs, then up and over his shoulder. He was now straddling the rope. He took the leftover rope and gripped it with his gloved hands right near his hip. Mom, watching all this, realized what he was doing. "It's the Dulfersitz technique," she said, "one of the oldest methods for self-rappel."

The ranger descended his rope while carrying a pack with him. With precision control, he dropped down to just above the snow cave.

The ranger stopped his descent abruptly above the cave. There he stayed on rope and tested his weight on the lip of the ice, making sure it could withstand any pressure. Once the ranger finished making the area more secure, he planted an ice ax into the snow above the cave. Then he secured the rope to the ice ax and lowered himself to where Greg and Cameron were trapped below.

Dad jogged up to Morgan, James, and Mom. "That was sure quick!" Mom said with surprise.

"Going downhill is a lot easier than up," Dad replied.

The ranger appeared to care for both Greg and Cameron, although much of Greg's body remained out of sight. The sky had clouded up again, and a few tiny sprinkles began to come down.

Mom felt a drop of rain on her nose. She looked up at ominous conditions, especially at this elevation, around ten thousand feet. Mom ignored the weather and watched the ranger administer to Greg and Cameron.

More rain fell, this time in significantly larger drops.

"It might be best to get to camp ourselves before another round of thunderstorms breaks loose," Mom said. "I'd hate to be caught on the trail if what happened yesterday strikes again. And we still have a good distance to go."

Dad agreed with Mom. "We'd better keep moving and stay warm. I don't think there's anything more we can do here anyway. They're in good hands now."

The Parkers left the moraine side trail and began hiking down Cascade Canyon. At first they each kept turning around and reporting what they could see of the rescue. But that didn't last long. A few switchbacks farther down, James said, "I can't see anything anymore."

As the family continued down into the deep canyon, it was still cloudy with occasional spritzes of showers, but the conditions improved. Temperatures were warmer, too.

The family hiked along, trying to take in the now-lush plant growth. Waterfalls and cascades plunged down from side canyons and snowfields above. Still, with their minds fixed on what happened at Schoolroom Glacier, James said, "I really wish we knew if they're going to be OK."

Eventually Morgan, James, Mom, and Dad came to a junction in the trail and began climbing into the next designated camping zone, below Lake Solitude and Paintbrush Divide.

It's a Climb

The Parkers were now well into California, heading down Highway 5, south toward San Luis Obispo.

"Recording all this sure makes the time pass quickly," Morgan said. "Soon we'll be home. We better finish telling the vacation while we can."

And with that, Morgan began recounting the next leg of their high-country journey.

"We got up fairly early," Morgan recalled, "and started packing our campsite in the north part of Cascade Canyon. We'd been watching the slopes high above for animals, but so far we hadn't seen any."

As the Parkers were finishing breakfast, a ranger came by. She pointed out the trail that the family would soon be on, far above. The Parkers grabbed their binoculars and could see a line of people passing by some stunted trees near the top of the mountain. "That is one long way up," Dad said.

"It's just going to have to be one foot in front of the other," Mom said, "one step at a time."

"By the way," the ranger said, "a black bear was seen in this campsite a few days ago. But there were no reports of any problems. Did you see or hear anything?"

The Parkers all looked at each other, realizing they just spent a night in the backcountry with a possible bear nearby. "No bears that we were aware of," Dad said.

After the ranger left, James and Morgan went down to the creek to filter water. The gurgling, cascading stream drowned out any chance that their parents would hear them if a bear ambled through the thick plants at streamside. Mom and Dad gave the twins one of the bear spray canisters to take along.

Once they finished pumping, Morgan and James gathered up their stuff and saw Dad standing there. "I wanted to make sure all was OK," Dad said, then smiled.

But James, who was already hiking back, called out, "Hey! Look!"

Dad's and Morgan's hearts jumped instinctively, as if it was a bear.

James was pointing up a tree, but without a sense of urgency.

Two squirrels had scampered to the very top of the tree, and a pine marten was climbing up after them!

The marten, coolly and calmly, as if it had done this hundreds of times, made it to the top branch, where the two squirrels were trapped. There was no tree nearby they could jump to!

The marten instantly lurched forward and bit into a loudly protesting squirrel. The carnivore then scampered back down with its prey twisting and screeching in its mouth.

"Wow!" James exclaimed.

"Gruesome," said Morgan. "That poor squirrel. But I guess that's nature."

Morgan, James, and Dad walked back to camp and told Mom about the encounter. After hearing the details of the pine marten squirrel hunt, Mom said, "I wish I would have seen that!"

Then all four Parkers finished cleaning up their campsite and loading their packs. Once they started walking, the trail was a relentless climb.

"And more of a climb," James said.

"It went on and on," Mom added. "But at least the views kept getting better and better!"

"Dad, you said somewhere up there that we were getting only the views that clouds get," James recalled.

Dad smiled. "I think that sounds kind of poetic!"

"Eventually we passed the stunted trees section we picked out with binoculars earlier," James said.

"That's where we saw and heard pikas!" Morgan exclaimed. "I even saw one scamper away with a clump of grass in its mouth. They look like little rabbits, and you have to admit, they're adorable."

"Well, they are part of the rabbit family," Mom said. "But it was good to see them up there. Pikas are homebodies. They basically stay within one area their whole life. But global warming has forced their habitat into only the higher mountain areas of the West. Below certain elevations, it is just too warm for them. They need to be where it is always

less than seventy-two degrees, and places like that are getting harder and harder for them to find."

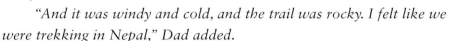

"We sure were on the high peaks area ourselves by then," Morgan added. "We could see snowfields, frozen lakes, and bare rocky summits all around us."

"And it was windy and cold, and the trail was rocky. I felt like we were trekking in Nepal," Dad added.

"Finally we saw a group of people at a summit sign ahead. That got us moving faster. I remember saying 'The end is near!'" James recalled.

"The top of the pass was 10,700 feet," Dad recalled. "No wonder we felt light-headed."

"Soon after, Mom, you looked at Dad and said, 'I have no idea how we're going to climb over three thousand feet higher than this! I don't

even know if it's possible,'" Morgan said, then continued. "After lunch at the pass, we bundled up. It was really cold up there! We hiked down—*a nice word to finally say!—some pretty nasty switchbacks. The trail was steep and rocky."*

"Remember that person who got scared coming up the side we were going down?" James reminded everyone. "He was stuck there, not moving."

"His friend had to drop both their packs off at the top and come back to try and get him over the summit," Mom added.

"I hope he made it," Dad said.

"But, thankfully, we did," Mom continued. "We camped in the upper Paintbrush area that night. The next day was a long *descent all the way back to our waiting car at the String Lake and Leigh Lake trailhead."*

"It was sad to be back down in some ways, sad to leave the wilderness," Dad said.

"That's exactly how I felt," Morgan added. "And still do! Couldn't we extend our trip, somewhere, by a few weeks?"

The View from Below

After a quick stop to fill up the car with gas and stretch their legs, the family was back on the road. "My turn!" James announced.

"OK," Morgan replied. James took the tape recorder.

"It was late evening when Grandma and Grandpa showed up. They were exhausted, so after hugs and hellos, they went to sleep in the cabin next door to us. We all had early starts the next day.

"Mom and Dad tried to sneak out quietly just before one in the morning but Morgan and I heard them, and Grandma came over to stay with us. Anyway, we couldn't let Mom and Dad go without saying good-bye. 'Good-bye, Mom and Dad—see you soon,' we all said, hugging them in the middle of the night as if they were going on a journey to the moon.

"'Remember, we'll be watching you up there,' I said. 'Be careful,' Grandma said, looking stern and serious. Truthfully, Morgan and I were nervous, too. I mean, we'd been looking at the rock-strewn Grand Teton for over a week now, and it was quite a peak. But we didn't want to say anything.

"After saying good-bye, we all tried to get some sleep. But I think Mom and Dad were on all our minds. Eventually I dozed off a little until our alarm clock went off some time after five in the morning.

"We went out on the Snake River early for the sunrise float trip. It was cold at dawn, but our large raft kept us out of the water and dry the *whole time. We didn't even have to paddle. And the river was calm and peaceful, gently flowing along.*

"Our guide talked a lot about the wolves being back in the area and how for some that was great, making the Greater Yellowstone Ecosystem complete. But for others wolves are a problem, causing ranchers to be concerned for their stock animals.

THE GREATER YELLOWSTONE ECOSYSTEM

The Greater Yellowstone Ecosystem is one of the last remaining large natural areas on the planet that still has a complete assembly of key wildlife species present and subsisting in it. The area includes Yellowstone and Grand Teton National Parks as well as six surrounding national forests, three wildlife refuges, and some state and private lands. This makes for over twenty-two million acres of preserved land, an incredible wildlife habitat and the largest essentially intact ecosystem outside of Alaska.

"For us, wolves had been the one animal, so far, that had eluded us. But, hey, the trip wasn't exactly over.

"And neither was the float trip, our animal highlight being a bald eagle flying from its nest right overhead. I ducked when it went by,

although I am not sure it was really that close. Everyone quickly snapped photos until the bird swooped out of sight.

"We also saw swallows and Canada geese with their babies and a pronghorn off in the distance. And there were five flying pelicans! But Morgan and I kept glancing

over to the Grand Teton, when we could see it, wondering where our parents were at that time.

"After the river trip, we hurried over to Jenny Lake Lodge. As soon as we got there, Grandpa said, 'I remember this place! We stayed here on our honeymoon!'"

Grandma responded with a smile. "That was so long ago, I thought you forgot."

Grandpa looked back and said, "Never! Me?!"

After the bantering, Grandpa took his spotting scope to the deck and zoomed in on the top of the Grand. A few other people nearby were doing the same.

Grandpa focused in on the mountain. The weather was bright and clear—a perfect day, or at least so it appeared from his vantage point. He could clearly see the summit.

At 10:15 a.m. James called out, "I can see people up there!" He passed the spotting scope to Morgan, who took a good look before handing it back to her grandparents.

Sure enough, there was a group of people hanging around at the very top of the Grand. At first they couldn't make out any more details, as at times the mountaineers were out of sight, disappearing behind some rocks. Other times, though, they could clearly see the climbers. "I wonder what techniques they all used to get up there," James said, picturing under-clings and mantles, among other maneuvers.

A few minutes later, Grandma nearly screamed, "It's them! I can see their red jackets!"

Morgan peered into the spotting scope and found what she thought was Mom and Dad. Her heart raced. They were on top of the mountain, red jackets and all.

Finally Mom and Dad, or at least who the Parkers down below thought were Mom and Dad, appeared to clasp and raise their hands right on the pinnacle of the Grand!

Morgan and James raised their arms in triumph, too, while keeping the spotting scope set on the mountain. "Hi, Mom and Dad," Morgan called out and waved. "Congratulations!"

"Hi, Mom. Hi, Dad!" James echoed. "You made it, whoo-hoo!"

Morgan and James again waved to their parents.

"I think they just waved back," James said, hoping that it was true.

Just then, Grandpa's cell phone jingled. He opened it up and read a text message.

> At summit of Grand. MOST AMAZING VIEW EVER! All is
> well, but very tired. It will take a LONG TIME to get down.
> See you at dinner. Love, Mom+Dad

"Why didn't they just call?" Grandma said, but then she looked at the twins, who appeared to have tears in their eyes.

On Top of the World

The Parkers were now about an hour away from home. James passed the tape recorder up to Mom and Dad. "I know you both can't wait to share your details of summiting the Grand," he said.

"You are certainly right about that," Dad said and started.

"We were up, as you know, before 1:00 a.m. I don't think I slept at all that night. Maybe an hour, but even that was extremely restless." Dad paused for a second. "Thanks for seeing us out the door, by the way."

James and Morgan smiled. "You're welcome."

Dad continued. "We met our guide, Andy, at the Exum office near Jenny Lake. After getting shoes, our helmets, and checking our clothing, food, and water, we drove to the trailhead a short distance away."

Mom took over. "We began our quest at 1:30 a.m. It was, for us, going to be a one-day summit of North America's most famous peak. Most people make the journey in two. As we hiked during the night, I often wondered what we were doing up there when we could be asleep. 'Shouldn't we be in bed?' I said to Dad at one point."

"But we kept a brisk pace, while sleep-hiking," Dad said jokingly. "And I think it was good to not see all the scenery where we were going. I know we were steadily climbing, that's for sure. And the trail kept getting steeper and steeper. I remember how loud my breathing often was. I didn't talk much to save my breath."

Mom added, "At 4:00 a.m. we stopped at a spring. Water was gushing out of the mountain and we drank right from it. It was so cold up there. Now we could also see the headlamps of people above and below us. We weren't alone.

"Soon after, Andy had us don our helmets. And we scaled several ropes fixed into the rock in a particularly steep area. Funny," Mom mused, "we were rock climbing at night using only headlamps for light. I wonder when I'll ever be able to say that again."

"Not anytime soon, anyway," Dad responded. "After the ropes, the light we saw far above was from the Exum hut at 11,600 feet. We were getting there and plowed on."

Mom and Dad finally made it to the hut. They were both shivering and cold. Particularly Dad, who had sweated so much during the five thousand feet of climbing they had done so far. Once they got inside, Dad had to immediately shed the soaked attire he had on.

"Here, let me help you unzip your jacket," Mom said as she watched Dad struggle to move his fingers.

"Thanks," Dad replied. "I can't even use my hands right now." But once Dad had on warm, dry clothes, he quickly recovered. Then Andy got both Mom and Dad hot water with electrolytes mixed in.

"You both should get some food in you," Andy said.

Mom took a bite out of an energy bar. "I don't really have an appetite," she reported. "My system is all out of whack."

Mom and Dad looked around the tiny hut. There was room in there for fifteen to twenty people in tight quarters. Sleeping gear was

strewn about but everyone was gone, heading up the mountain. Dad said, "It looks like we're at an Everest base camp."

Mom and Dad put on an extra layer of warm, dry clothes then put their jackets back on. They stepped outside. Dawn was just beginning to break. Once out, they could see for the first time the rockbound world they were in. And then they looked up.

"Oh my God!" Dad gawked when seeing massive Grand Teton towering almost directly above. It was incredibly imposing to the first-time-mountaineer Parkers. "We still have over two thousand feet of climbing to go, too!" Dad added.

"That is one colossal feat waiting," Mom replied.

A few minutes later, they were hiking up. Dad felt his breathing starting to labor. The altitude and the steepness of the hike were really getting to him. He had to stop and rest over and over.

Soon they were in an area Andy called "Idaho Express." It was incredibly steep. Andy said, "When there's snow in there, which there often is, if you fall you'll be swept all the way to Idaho."

"Thankfully there is no snow in there now," Dad said.

Andy and Mom and Dad kept climbing, and while they did, Andy told them the names for each section on the mountain. They passed the Black Dike, The Needle, Briggs Slab, and the Upper Saddle, and were eventually on the Owen-Spalding route, one of the original ways up the Grand.

"At times the terrain was completely vertical and Andy had us rope up," Mom said. "I remember one section was called the Belly Roll and another, the Crawl."

"I think," Dad said, "that's where I nearly lost it. Here we were, crawling through a fairly tight passage, straddling rocks along the way, and all with a massive drop-off immediately on our left. I'm guessing it

was two thousand or so feet straight down. That's what I recall, anyway. It was incredibly exposed."

"We just couldn't, or didn't, think that was the key to our ascent," Mom said. *"And Andy just kept us moving, too, so that helped.*

"Soon," Mom went on, *"we made it to what Andy said was the 'crux' of our climb, the Owen Chimney. I looked up and thought, yes, I can do this!"*

"The climbing actually helped me," Dad said. *"Because of the rope work, we slowed down some. It gave me a chance to catch my breath. I mean I was breathing* hard *up there. But once we were scaling the chimney, my confidence surged. We both were doing it! And the rock had a ton of features to grip onto. I remember you called one of them,"* Dad said to Mom, *"a 'thank-God hold.'*

"After the Owen Chimney," Dad continued, *"a few more climbing spots awaited, and then we were short-roped, where Andy had us on a small leash, in case we slipped. Then, soon after, there we were, celebrating on the summit of the Grand!"*

"We're on top of the world!" Mom remembered shouting. *Then she said, "That was as breathtaking a view as I have ever seen."*

"Or perhaps we ever will see," Dad said. *"We could see lakes, glaciers, mountains, and even Jackson Hole Valley far, far below."*

"That's about when I decided to text Grandma and Grandpa," Mom said to the twins.

"We were at Jenny Lake with them!" James exclaimed. *"And we could see people at the summit with binoculars. But why didn't you just call?"*

"It was real windy at the top of the Grand and, believe it or not, quite a few people were all crowded into one small area up there. Dad and I didn't think we would be able to hear you, or we'd have to shout for you to hear us, so we just thought a written message was best at the time."

Morgan said, "We saw two people with red jackets. Was that you?"

"It could have been," Mom replied. "But, truthfully, there were quite a few people up there. And I kind of remember several others had red jackets on or at least bright clothing. So, really, it only might have been us."

"I want to remember it as we saw you," James said, "and you waved to us."

"I think that probably happened," Dad responded and turned to Mom with a sly wink. "We spent a few minutes at the very summit. We ate energy bars, drank water, high-fived, raised our arms in triumph, took pictures, and soaked it all in."

Dad continued, "Andy said at some point while we were up there, 'You know, this whole climb to the top of the Grand was optional. But now that we are here, climbing down isn't. Are you ready?'"

"Once we said yes to Andy," Mom added, "we began the slow, incredibly tedious process of going down the mountain, knowing any misstep could result in serious injury, or worse."

"Still," Dad recalled, "I remember saying after a short while on the descent, 'This is easier for me. My lungs aren't working so hard.'"

Mom said, "There were obstacles on every step up there: loose rock, boulders, snow patches, and all of that in steep terrain. We knew it was going to take a long *time to get down.*"

"At one point Andy rappelled us over a big ledge. It was like we were back at Hidden Falls," Dad said. "Eventually we made it back to the Exum hut, and then it was a whole new ball game. The day was bright and warm, and a lot less windy. I even had to shed clothes. And we both were able to finally down some breakfast."

"And remember," Mom added, "massive Middle Teton Glacier was just below the hut. I can't believe we hiked right by that in the middle of the night."

"That's what I kept thinking about on the whole way down," Dad said. "Seeing the things we missed during the night, like that glacier's bergschrunds, *was amazing.*"

"And," Mom added, "remember the stream of water that was streaming right out of the ice?

"We kept on going down the mountain trail," Mom continued. "There was also that fixed-rope area in the daylight, and massive jumbles of boulders to cross, but eventually we made it back to the land of trees."

"We saw lots of pikas, too," Dad said. "But that spring—it was the cleanest, freshest, coldest, best-tasting water I think I've ever had. I guzzled three or four bottles of it right on the spot!"

"The meadows area was so lush and wet below the snowfields and glacier," Mom recalled. "I think that was the most scenic spot for me."

"At times the trail was clear, too, and not always boulders and rocks," Dad said. "Still, there were plenty more obstacles to come. Eventually, though, we were on the Surprise and Amphitheater Lakes trail."

"And that included those never-ending switchbacks down," Mom added.

"Mom and I were both feeling better," Dad continued. "Going lower gave us more oxygen. But, boy, that trail was long!"

"It felt like someone had stretched it out during the night," Mom said. "It took forever."

"I knew we were getting close when we reached that silted stream near the bottom," Dad said. "I dipped my hat in the water and realized that it, too, was from a glacier up above. It was a little cloudy and very cold. But who would have thought that I actually needed to cool down after I was so cold earlier that morning?"

"Finally," Mom emphasized, "we made it to our car, exhausted but content. We drove to the office, and there they made us one of these!"

Mom fished out of the glove compartment an Exum certificate with Robert and Kristen Parker's Grand Teton accomplishment listed on it.

"We returned our gear and said good-bye to Andy and all the folks at Exum," Mom continued. "'Nice climbing, you two,' Andy said with a big smile that said he was proud to be our leader."

"Then," Dad said while taking a deep breath as he remembered, "we drove to find Grandma and Grandpa at the Jackson Lake Lodge."

"They took off for Yellowstone, and for us it was day of well-deserved luxury," Mom said.

"Except," Dad joked, "I think I slept through most of it."

Morgan asked Mom and Dad, "Would you do it again?"

Mom paused to think. "Maybe, yes," she replied. "But Dad and I agreed, only with the two of you. In a few years."

"Deal!" James said. And the Parkers all touched fists to seal the agreement.

Something We All Deserve

"This one's for all of us to tell," Mom announced while driving.

The family was now approaching the Cuesta Grade, just outside of San Luis Obispo, and nearly home.

Dad picked up the recorder and announced, "Our final Teton memory on the Elk Island Dinner Cruise as told by all of us." He then began: "We went to the Colter Bay Marina, where there was a large gathering of people, including many families, waiting for the boat to Elk Island."

"I remember reading somewhere that Colter Bay was named after John Colter, a member of the Corps of Discovery, also called the Lewis and Clark expedition of 1804 to 1806," James said. "Colter explored the Teton area in the winter of 1807 to 1808."

"Good memory!" Morgan said. "I remember that our boat was named Teewinot, after one of the mountains we'd been seeing all week. I like how the host said the many peaks on it looked like stegosaurus plates."

"Once water-bound," Mom went on, "the lake looked so calm and peaceful. And the peaks were mirrored in the water."

"The host pointed out Skillet Glacier on Mount Moran," Morgan added, "and said that although it is called a skillet, it really is shaped like a guitar."

"Yeah," James said. "And with all the rocks surrounding it, the glacier is part of a rock band!"

Morgan smiled. "Well, I guess some of the host's jokes worked better than others."

The family laughed.

Mom continued the story. "The host also mentioned that people climb the mountains in the Tetons every day of the year, even when they are completely filled with snow."

"I'm glad we didn't have to deal with snow and ice," Dad said. "But when I heard that, it made me think of Greg and Cameron. I remember feeling relieved and concerned when we read the press release and knew they were taken by helicopter to a hospital. We haven't heard a thing since then, though. I wonder how they are doing. Were they badly injured? How long were they up there?"

"I think we are all still worried," Mom said.

"Hopefully we can find out how they are doing once we get home," James said. "Maybe we can call the hospital."

After a moment of silence, Morgan continued the story. "The host said to all the kids on the boat that one day we would come back and take our parents to Grand Teton National Park."

Dad smiled. "I'm all for that."

"Remember when we got to the island," James said, "as the host helped us step off the boat, he announced, 'Welcome to Jurassic Park!'"

Morgan smiled. "Yeah, we looked at each other, then at the island, expecting to see a dinosaur grazing nearby."

"I don't know about 'expecting,'" James said. "But maybe hoping!"

"It was quite a little spread of food they had out there, too," Mom recalled. "But we certainly needed those calories after all the energy we expended up in the mountains. By the way, what was your favorite food?"

"The seasoned trout!"

"Buttered corn on the cob."

"Stir-fried potatoes."

"Fresh salad."

"Dessert!" the Parkers all announced at once.

Morgan and James laughed.

"I think food cooked outdoors always tastes better anyway," Dad said.

James started, "It was interesting to learn that moose, elk, deer, and bears sometimes walk out to Elk Island when the lake is frozen over in winter, and they can swim out to the island in the summer."

"Imagine seeing a bear swimming out there alongside the boat," Dad mused.

Mom added, "Deer and elk have hollow fur, making them buoyant."

Morgan thought for a second. "It took us about an hour to get out there by boat!"

"Then it was time for us to leave," Mom said. "That was hard because we all wanted to stay and explore the beautiful island we were on!"

"But at least there was that one final surprise on the boat ride back," Dad said. He paused and let the twins take over the story.

"The bull elk!" Morgan called out.

"There were three of them right on the bluff at the edge of the island," James added.

"The captain steered the boat closer so we could all get a better look and take pictures," Morgan said. "Their antlers were huge. And I could see the velvet on them."

"They were just sitting in the grass like they were posing for us," James said.

Morgan and James soon ran out of details. Finally Mom said, "I don't know about you guys, but that capped my trip."

"Mine, too," the rest of the family agreed.

A Surprise in the Mail

On August 30 a large, heavy box arrived via US Mail at the Parkers' home in San Luis Obispo. It had a Georgia return address on it, but no name. An envelope taped to the outside of the box read "To Morgan, James, Robert, and Kristen."

All four of the Parkers looked at the box eagerly. "Let's read the letter first," Morgan directed. She grabbed the envelope and tore it open. Inside was a card with the Tetons on it and three sets of notes.

Morgan looked at her family. "I'm going to read this one, OK?"

> Dear Morgan, James, Robert, and Kristen,
>
> After being hoisted out of the ice cave, I was taken by helicopter from Schoolroom Glacier. I spent several days in a hospital with a concussion and multiple cuts, bruises, and abrasions. I also had hypothermia, but that passed quickly. It is still hard to recall all the details of that day. I was unconscious part of the time, too. As it turned out, I didn't get hurt all that badly. But, truly, if it weren't for all the help I got up there, including, I hear, from you, I may not have made it back into high school, as I am now, and pretty much recovered. Please accept this gift from Cameron and me as a token of our gratitude and for possibly saving my life.
>
> Sincerely,
> Greg Wright

James took the card from Morgan and read the second note out loud.

Dear Morgan, James, Kristen, and Robert,

Like my older brother, Greg, I too was airlift rescued and hospitalized, but just overnight. It was quite a little pulley system the backcountry rangers set up to haul Greg and me out of there. I wish I could have watched it all and not been the reason for it. Funny, though, once at the hospital, Greg recovered faster, but seemed at the time to be hurt worse. I'm still hobbling around with a cast on my leg. I broke my tibia bone, as well as got a nasty cut on my forehead, but the doctor says I'll make a full recovery, and you know what that means? The Teton Crest Trail next summer! Do you want to join Greg and me? Or maybe we'll scale the Grand!? Greg and I so appreciate how you helped us out of our hole, literally!

Sincerely,

Cameron Wright

PS—We thought you might like what is in the box.

There was one more note in the card. Mom and Dad looked at each other, then Kristen took it.

To the Parker family,

We are so grateful for what you did to help our sons. Please accept what we have sent as the utmost reflection of our thanks. And, also know that if you are ever in Macon, Georgia, we definitely want you to come stay with us (and to show us your photos of your Teton adventures!).

Sincerely,

Dana and Charles Wright

PS—We got your information from the accident report and looked you up. I hope that was OK.

After reading the notes, all four Parkers looked at each other. "I'm so glad to hear that they are better," Dad said.

The family turned their attention to the box. Mom dashed to their office and grabbed some scissors. She sliced open the tape, and the Parkers each yanked out some of the paper stuffing and Styrofoam packaging.

"It's a backpack!" James exclaimed.

It was a big, blue, brand-new one with all kinds of pouches and storage areas. "Wow!" Dad said. "This sure has all the bells and whistles."

"It's for you, Dad," James said. "All of ours are fairly new."

Dad hoisted the pack out of the box. "It's heavy!" he exclaimed.

Out of curiosity, Dad unzipped one of the pouches. He reached in and pulled out a handful of energy bars. "Whoa!" he said.

Morgan opened another pouch and pulled out a compass. "Look!" she said, then she grabbed a whistle, mini flashlight, and waterproof matches out of the same compartment.

James opened another zipper and found two emergency ponchos and a small rope. "Another treasure!" he announced.

Dad then found some stashed hot cocoa packages and some socks.

Mom found a compartment with a small first-aid kit.

The Parkers piled up their gifts, but the pack still felt bulky.

Dad reached into the main storage area and pulled out a carefully wrapped rectangular-shaped object.

Dad unwrapped the last gift. It was a framed photograph of Greg and Cameron giving a thumbs-up with the Teton mountains skyline looming in the background. It was taken at Colter Bay.

"Wow!" Mom said as a tear trickled down her face . . .